"Oncology, Stupc
I want to go home!"

Story by Marilyn K. Hershey
Pictures by Jill M. Thomas

Butterfly Press

ISBN # 0-9673550-0-1, copyright© 1999 by Butterfly Press, Marilyn K. Hershey

To order copies of *Oncology Stupology . . . I want to go home!* visit our web page www.butterfly-press.com
or call 888-593-5998

This book started as a small dream and with each bit of encouragement my dream grew. So many have helped develop my dream into reality. For this, I am truly grateful.

To the doctors and nurses at Penn State Geisinger Children's Hospital,
     you became our family.

To the Child Life Staff,
     your patience and love pulled us through.

To all those who believed in my dream and encouraged me,
     Dr. Bernie Siegel, Joy Johnson/Centering Corporation, Mary Ellen,
     Mary Wishneski, Diann Spangenberg, and my writers group.

To Sara Davis,
     for all your hours of help – I couldn't have done it with out you!

To Jill,
     for bringing my book to life.

To Duane
     for trusting me enough to dream with me.

To Joyce,
     for never letting me give up. You are a true friend.

                              God's Peace to you
                                        —Marilyn

To Marilyn and Robert,
     for asking me to be a part of your touching story.

To my friends and family,
     for all your encouragement, especially my Mom, who is with me in spirit.

To Darrek,
     for bringing out the best in me and my artwork.
     I can't thank you enough for all of your help with this project.

                                        —Jill

This book is for
every child,
young and old,
who battles cancer.
Especially for
the bravest of them all –

Robert and Kyle.

My body hurt and I was tired. I felt bad. Real bad.
My mom took me to the doctor.

"You're sick," the doctor said.

"Well duh!" I said.

He said I'd go to the hospital for lots of medicine.
It would make me sick in my head and sick in my stomach.
I would even lose my hair – for a little while.

"What is it?" I asked.

"You have cancer," he said.

The important people call it **Oncology**
I call it Oncology Stupology . . . and I want to stay home!

My mom and I packed for the hospital.
I packed my special pillow, my teddy bear, and my really cool pajamas.
My mom packed enough stuff to stay forever.

"Good grief," I said.

When I got there, all the
important people were waiting.
They gave me a room
with a bed and a TV.
It even had a cot for my mom.
A nurse hooked me up
to a tube called an IV.
Then the tests started.
    They tested my insides . . .
    tested my outsides . . .
    tested all my sides.
They especially tested my blood.
I told them, "if you take
any more blood from me, I'm
going to look like a raisin!

    Oncology is Stupology . . .
    I want to go home!"

My friends came to see me.
They brought balloons and all kinds of stuff
to make me feel better. Sometimes it did.
Sometimes it didn't!

My Dad came too.
We played video games, watched TV
and talked about car races.

The nurse hung my chemo, (the stuff that makes my hair fall out).
   "Time for your medicine, Tiger," she said.
It was **always** time for my medicine
and the nurse **always** called me Tiger.

She put the medicine thru my IV.
It looked orange - just like fruit drink. It didn't feel like fruit drink.
    "Push the nurse button if you need me Tiger," she said.
    BE-BE-BEEP, BE-BE-BEEP, I pushed. BE-BE-BE-BE-BEEP.

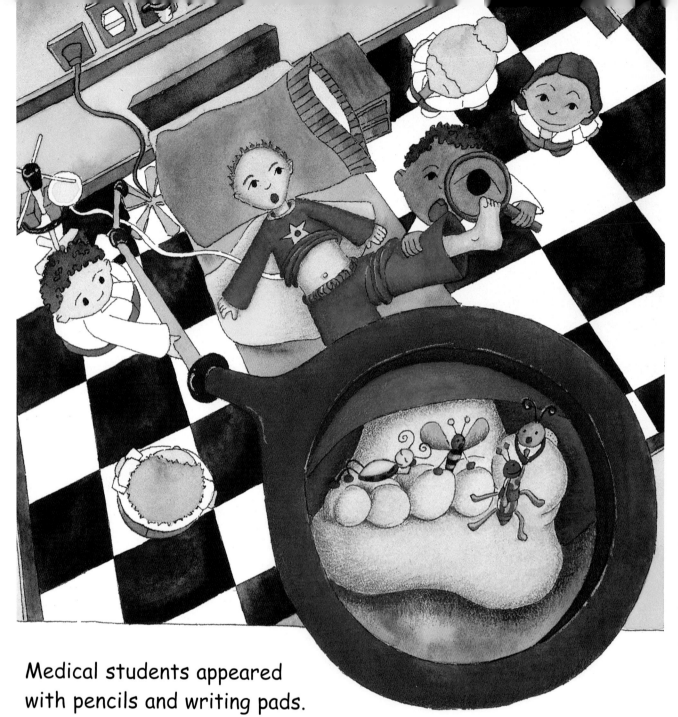

Medical students appeared
with pencils and writing pads.
They asked a lot of questions and took a lot of notes.
 "How much did you weigh on your first birthday?"
 "How many times have you sneezed in your life?"
 "Is your belly button an inny or an outty?"
They even wanted to know how much dirt I hid under my toenails.
 "Do you know?" I asked them.
 "If Oncology is Stupology, when can I go home?"

The lunch lady brought a tray of supposed-to-be food.

"Time to eat," she said.

"Did I order this dry burger and soggy fries?" I asked.
I wonder . . . if I throw it out the window,
will it bounce back up to the seventh floor?
Maybe more ketchup will help.

I walked down the hall, pulling my IV pole behind me.
It had squeaky wheels.
Everyone held their ears when I walked past.
I walked to the big wide window.
I could look outside and see real far.

I saw the miniature cars and ant-like people.
I saw tall buildings and far-away factories.
I even saw a Ferris Wheel spinning in the nearby park.

     "That's where I want to be," I said. "Out there, where there's
no more Oncology, Stupology . . . I want to go home."

I felt tired. My squeaky pole and I walked back to bed.
My head sank into my special pillow. AAHHHH!! It felt so good.
While I slept the cleaning lady snuck in.
    "HOUSEKEEPING" she screeched!
It woke the whole hospital.
I grumbled as she mopped the floor-including my shark slippers.

The Child Life person came to read me a book.
She brought my favorite story.
I buried my face in my pillow and pretended not to care.
She read the whole book!   I only peeked twice.

"Oncology is Stupology . . . but can you read that again?"

My mom stayed with me in the hospital.
She fluffed my pillow, brought me favorite snacks,
fetched my shark slippers and ate my horrible lunches.
Most of all she answered the telephone.
She loved talking on the telephone.
She told everyone that Oncology is Stupology.

The aide took my temperature and checked my blood pressure.
It was the millionth time that day.

"Hold your tongue still," he said.

"And don't move your arm. It'll just be a minute."

I stood still as a rock.

"Oncology, Stupology," I mumbled-without moving my tongue.

"I want to go home."

I had great fun with my nurse.
Sometimes we played soccer in the hallway.

One time we actually had a water battle. She lost!

The Child Life lady showed me a great toy.
"There are lots more in the playroom," she said.

I pulled my squeaky pole to the playroom.
  "Wow!" Toys, puzzles and games were everywhere!
Oncology is still Stupology . . . but this playroom is SO COOL!

I met this neat guy singing crazy songs.
He made me laugh.
I also met a friend named Chad.

Chad and I had a lot of fun together. He was just like me.
His IV pole squeaked.
He had no hair and he agreed – Oncology **is** Stupology . . .
Chad wants to go home too.

Weeks went by . . .
  more medicine,
  more blood work,
  still no hair.
Then one day during his
rounds . . .
  the doctor came in.
Everyone bowed.
Except me.
  "Your blood counts
  are up," he said.
  "Maybe you can
  get out of here for
  a couple of weeks."

I packed my
teddy bear and balloons.
I packed my really
cool pajamas and
special pillow.
I packed my
shark slippers.
I packed my mom!
The car was stuffed so full,
I almost didn't fit.

"Have fun nurse," I said.
"See you later Chad.
Good bye doctor," I yelled.
    "Oncology may be Stupology,"
    "But I'm going home!"

And I did.

"Natives live an experience. Doctors treat a diagnosis and are tourists. Let a natives experience help prepare you or a loved one."

Dr. Bernie Siegel, MD
author
Love, Medicine & Miracles,
Prescriptions for Living

"This book is really cool!, I want my own copy."
Tanner, age 7
Receiving chemotherapy
for Leukemia.

Marilyn, Robert and Jill

Marilyn lives with her family in Southeastern Pennsylvania (husband Duane, children: Steve, Kelby, Robert, and Kacie.) Robert finished treatment for Leukemia in January, 1998.

Jill lives with her husband Darrek in Southeastern Pennsylvania.

ISBN 0-9673550-0-1

9 780967 355009   90000

SAMMY
THE
GOOD SPORT

Written by
TIFFANY OBENG
Illustrated by
ERIS ARUMAN

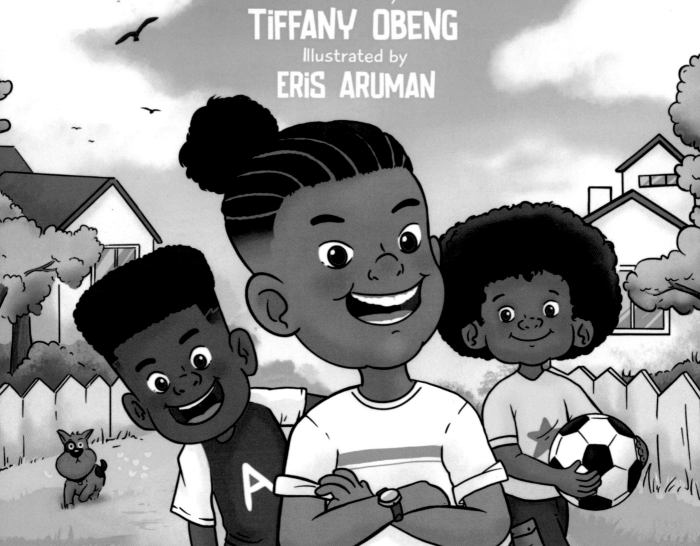